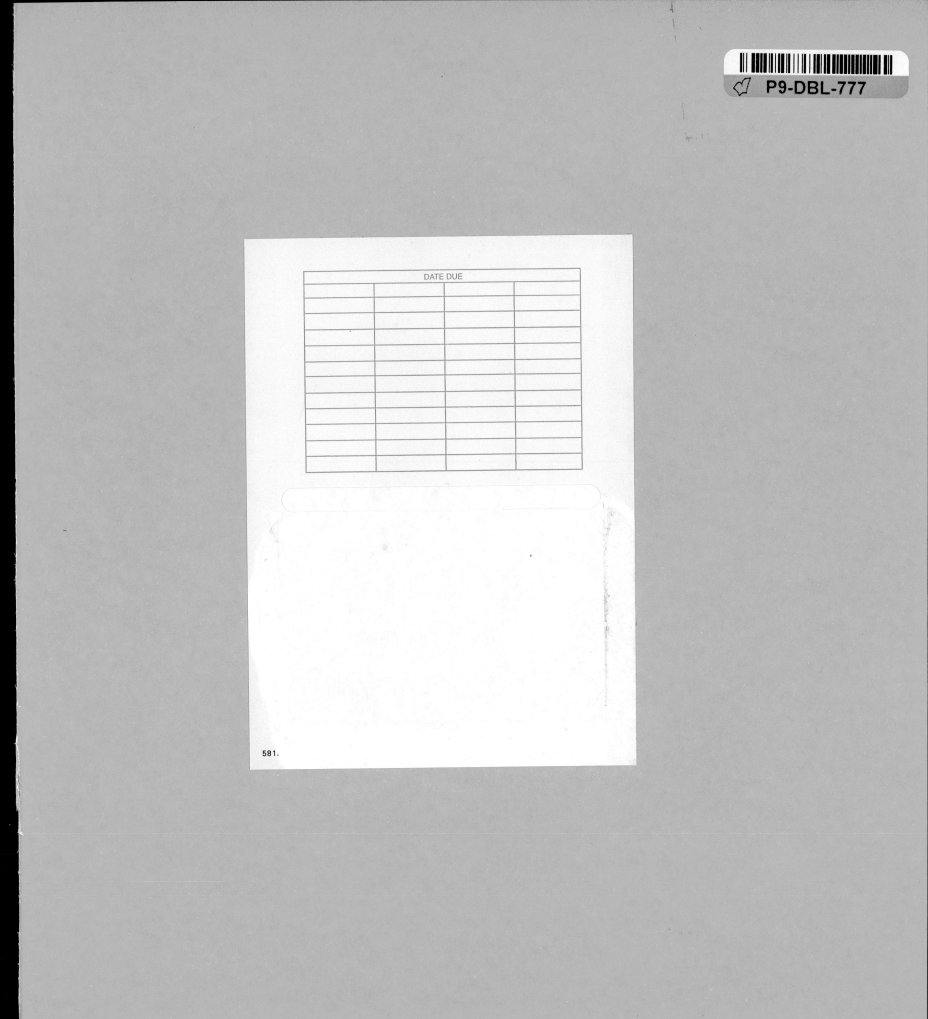

DATE DUE

In the Moonlight Mist

A Korean Tale

Retold by Daniel San Souci

Illustrated by Eujin Kim Neilan

Boyds Mills Press

Published by Caroline House
Boyds Mills Press, Inc.
A Highlights Company
815 Church Street
Honesdale, Pennsylvania 18431

Printed in China

Publisher Cataloging-in-Publication Data

San Souci, Daniel.
In the moonlight mist : a Korean tale / retold by Daniel San Souci ;
illustrated by Eujin Kim Neilan.—1st edition.
[32]p. : col. ill. ; cm.
Summary: A good-hearted woodcutter finds a heavenly wife in this retelling of a Korean folk tale.
ISBN 1-56397-754-0
1. Folklore—Korea—Juvenile literature [1. Folklore—Korea.] I. Neilan, Eujin Kim, ill. II. Title
398.2/09519 —dc21   1999 CIP
Library of Congress Catalog Card Number 98-73069

First edition, 1999
The text of this book is set in 16-point Berkeley.
The illustrations are done in acrylic.

10 9 8 7 6 5 4 3 2

To my loving niece, Monica Bischoff
—D. S. S.

To Alexia, my daughter, who brought me joy and luck
—E. K. N.

ONE SPRING AFTERNOON, a handsome young woodcutter put down his axe and started stacking freshly cut wood. Suddenly he heard a loud crackling in the distant underbrush. An instant later a deer bounded into the clearing in the trees and came to a halt.

"You must help me!" begged the animal, shaking with fright. "A hunter is chasing me. . . . He's going to kill me!"

"Follow me," said the woodcutter, who was a friend to all animals.
He led the deer behind a pile of wood and covered him with what branches
and leaves he could quickly gather. Then he returned to stacking wood.

Soon a husky hunter emerged from the trees.

"I seem to have lost the trail of a deer I've been following. Have you seen it?" he asked, looking from side to side.

"I did see the animal. He was headed toward the river," replied the woodcutter.

The hunter raced off toward the river with his bow and arrows ready.

As soon as he was out of sight the woodcutter called the deer from his hiding place.

"You saved my life," said the thankful deer. "I am a friend of the Mountain Spirit. You shall be rewarded for your kind deed."

"Just seeing you run free is reward enough," replied the woodcutter.

"Every man has a secret wish," the deer said. "Tell me yours and it shall be granted."

The woodcutter answered, "I've always dreamed of having a loving wife and children of my own, but I am poor and can barely take care of my aging mother and myself. Someday she will pass and the thought of living alone haunts me."

"This wish will be granted, but you must listen carefully to what I say," said the deer. "At the first full moon, climb to the crest of this mountain. There you will find a wall of vines with razor-sharp thorns. Take your axe and cut a path through these vines. Beyond, you will see a bewitching lake where heavenly maidens bathe under the full moon. While they are bathing, take one set of clothes, for without them, one maiden will not be able to return to heaven. She will see the goodness in you and will become your earthly wife."

"But how can I be loved by someone I have tricked?" asked the woodcutter.

"The Mountain Spirit will soften her heart," the animal replied. The deer paused for a moment and then said, "One last thing, woodcutter, do not give back her heavenly clothes until she bears your second child. Always remember these words."

Then the deer turned and bounded up the mountain slope.

When the woodcutter returned home that evening, he told his mother about the talking deer.

"Although it sounded sincere, I still have a hard time believing it," he told her.

"You are the finest son a mother could want," she responded. "It is time that you be rewarded for your hard work and devotion. My advice is to do exactly as you have been told."

For the next several days, the woodcutter went about his business of going into the woods and cutting firewood to bring home and sell.

Late one afternoon, as he was tying up the last bundle of wood, he noticed a hare sitting on its hind legs in a patch of clover.

"Go home and prepare yourself, for tonight there will be a full moon," said the hare. Then it hopped away.

That night, when a full moon appeared over the mountain, the woodcutter grabbed his axe and set out.

At the foot of the mountain he found a narrow path of moonlight that wound up the slopes. He followed the path all the way to the crest of the mountain. Below he could see the entire valley. Ahead stood a wall of tangled vines and thorns.

He started chopping at the vines and in a short time had cut a pathway to the other side. Beyond, he found a lake that looked like a giant mirror, reflecting the moon and stars. The woodcutter hid behind a large rock near the shore.

He saw what looked like five twinkling stars falling from the night sky. As they drew closer, he saw that they were beautiful maidens floating downward through the moonlit mist. Once they landed on shore, they undressed shyly behind a curtain of willow branches and hung their clothes on the lowest limb.

In the silent night the woodcutter heard five splashes and saw the maidens swim out to the middle of the lake, chatting loudly and laughing.

As the deer had told him to do, he stepped over to the tree and removed one set of the radiant clothes. He folded the garments and hid them under his jacket. He then returned to his hiding place.

When the first trace of morning light swept across the lake, the blissful maidens swam back to shore. But their good humor soon turned to distress.

"My clothes, where are my clothes?" cried one of the maidens desperately. "I will not be able to return to heaven without them!"

"They must be here somewhere, dear sister," replied another maiden.

But they searched in vain.

"You must keep on looking and join us later. We have run out of time," said another.

One by one, the maidens started rising into the sky. They sadly waved to their sister on the shore. Soon they vanished into the heavens.

The earth-bound maiden, her silky black hair covering her body like a robe, fell to her knees. She wept so sadly that the flowers around the lake started to wither.

"I will take care of you," said the woodcutter, slowly approaching her. "My mother will give you food to eat and clothes to wear."

She was frightened at first, but because the woodcutter seemed so kind and concerned, she decided to go home with him.

It didn't take her long to see that the woodcutter loved her deeply. Soon she fell in love with him and the two were married. While the woodcutter went to work, she stayed home and tended the garden and took care of his mother, who was growing very feeble.

At the end of their first year together they had a baby girl. Although the maiden was happy with her earthly life, she became homesick for heaven. One morning the woodcutter became concerned that his wife seemed depressed and asked, "What is wrong? Have I done something?"

"It's not your fault, dear husband," she said, sad-eyed. "I just miss my heavenly home and family."

"I wish there was something I could do to make you happy," he replied.

"If I could just see and feel my heavenly clothes, I'm sure it would make me happy again," she said.

The woodcutter went into the bedroom, pulled up a floorboard, retrieved the heavenly clothes, and handed them to his wife.

Although she intended only to look at and touch the garments, she became spellbound by the power they possessed and put them on. At that moment the baby in the crib cried. She lifted the baby and raced out of the house. By the time the woodcutter realized what was happening, his wife and baby were already floating up into the blue sky.

"Please come back home," he shouted in an agonized voice.

His wife and child floated higher and higher until they became a tiny speck in the sky, then they vanished completely.

The woodcutter's life became miserable. He spent all his time sleeping and feeling sorry for himself. One day he realized that there was no food in the house and his mother was half starved. Although he didn't feel up to it, he picked up his axe and headed off to chop firewood. When he reached the woods, he took a few swings with the axe but was soon overcome with painful thoughts. He sat down and stared into space.

"Hello, friend," spoke a familiar voice.

The woodcutter lowered his eyes and saw the deer right in front of him.

"You are not too good at following instructions, woodcutter!" said the deer.

"I was foolish," he said miserably. "Now my life is ruined."

"Every day that I run on this mountain and breathe the fresh air, I thank you for saving my life," said the deer. "There's no way I will let you suffer like this. Though the maidens no longer come down to earth to bathe since you stole your wife's clothes, when the moon is full they do lower a silver bucket into the lake to fill with water for their baths. Go to the lake tonight and climb inside the bucket, and you will be lifted to heaven to be reunited with your wife and child."

The deer then turned and vanished into the woodland.

That evening, the woodcutter was about to set off on his journey when he started to agonize over the thought of leaving his mother alone on earth. He decided the only way he could truly be happy was to take his mother to heaven with him. He picked up the frail woman and carried her all the way up the mountain, drawing strength from the thought that he'd soon be reunited with his wife and child.

When the bucket was lowered, he put his mother inside first and then climbed in himself. The bucket started to rise, but came to a sudden halt.

"There is too much weight, you must leave me here," said his mother.

Instead, the woodcutter jumped out of the bucket and watched as she was lifted into the air to heaven.

"You have lived a hard life, Mother. It's time you had some joy," he shouted to her.

When the heavenly king heard the story about how the woodcutter had sacrificed his own happiness for his mother's well-being, he decided that something should be done.

The following morning, the wood-cutter awoke to find a majestic winged dragon-horse waiting for him outside his house. With one look, he knew that the creature must have been sent from heaven. He mounted the dragon-horse and, within a blink of an eye, was in the heavenly kingdom.

The woodcutter was soon reunited with his wife, mother, and child. Their joy gave the moon and stars a luster that caused no end to the wonder on the earth below.